NINJA COWBOY BEAR PRESENTS

THE WAY OF THE
NINJA

For Esther — D.B.
For Naya — H.L.

Kids Can Press acknowledges the financial support of the Government of Ontario, through the Ontario Media Development Corporation's Ontario Book Initiative; the Ontario Arts Council; the Canada Council for the Arts; and the Government of Canada, through the BPIDP, for our publishing activity.

Published in Canada by
Kids Can Press Ltd.
29 Birch Avenue
Toronto, ON M4V 1E2

Published in the U.S. by
Kids Can Press Ltd.
2250 Military Road
Tonawanda, NY 14150

www.kidscanpress.com

The artwork in this book was rendered in Adobe Illustrator.
The text is set in Garamond.

Edited by Yvette Ghione
Designed by Hilary Leung

This book is smyth sewn casebound.
Manufactured in Singapore, in 3/2010 by Tien Wah Press (Pte) Ltd.

CM 10 0 9 8 7 6 5 4 3 2 1

The Japanese characters on page 13 are pronounced "Ho-shi o mezashi-te sora takaku tobi tatte iko" and those on page 19 "Kono asobi wa sora o tobimawaru yoh ni tanoshii yo." The sentences can be translated as "Let's shoot for the stars!" and "This game will be a fun flying experience!" respectively.

Library and Archives Canada Cataloguing in Publication

Bruins, David

    Ninja Cowboy Bear presents the way of the ninja / written by David Bruins ; illustrated by Hilary Leung.

ISBN 978-1-55453-615-3 (bound)

I. Leung, Hilary II. Title.

PS8603.R835N56 2010   jC813'.6   C2010-900207-5

www.ninja-cowboy-bear.com

FSC
Mixed Sources
Product group from well-managed forests, controlled sources and recycled wood or fibre
Cert no. DNV-COC-000025
www.fsc.org
© 1996 Forest Stewardship Council

NINJA COWBOY BEAR PRESENTS

THE WAY OF THE NINJA

David Bruins and Hilary Leung

Kids Can Press

The ninja loved to spend time with his friends the cowboy and the bear.

When they got together it usually led to
merrymaking, buffoonery and hilarity.

But not always. Sometimes they did not agree on what was fun.
The ninja had his own way of having fun. It often
included thrills and adventure.

One day his daring ways came between him and his friends ...

And here is what happened.

The ninja was bored and was looking for amusement.
So he went to see if the cowboy wanted to play.
The cowboy did. He wanted to paint pictures.

That did not sound like fun to the ninja. He wanted more thrills than that. The ninja convinced the cowboy that it would be more fun to jump on beds.

星を目指して空高く飛び立っていこう！

But the cowboy did not end up having fun at all.
The ninja thought the cowboy was being a poor sport.

So the ninja went to see if the bear wanted to play.
The bear did. He wanted to pick flowers.

That did not sound like fun to the ninja. He wanted more adventure than that. The ninja convinced the bear that it would be more fun to climb trees.

But the bear did not end up having fun at all.
The ninja thought the bear was overreacting.

The ninja decided that he would have to make his own fun.

But somehow it was not as exhilarating as usual.

Something was missing.

Then the ninja remembered that the greatest thrills and the best adventures were the ones he had shared with his friends. And he realized that he had acted carelessly.

Hoping his friends still wanted to play, the ninja went to find them.

When he did, he was thrilled to find that the cowboy did want to play.

And so did the bear.

And the three friends had more fun than ever.